D0466592

HOLD THEM CLOSE

A LOVE LETTER TO BLACK CHILDREN

WRITTEN BY
Jamilah Thompkins-Bigelow

ILLUSTRATED BY
Patrick Dougher

WITH PHOTOGRAPHY BY Jamel Shabazz

HARPER
An Imprint of HarperCollinsPublishers

Hold Them Close

Text copyright © 2022 by Jamilah Thompkins-Bigelow

Illustrations copyright © 2022 by Patrick Dougher

Photographs copyright © 2022 by Jamel Shabazz

All rights reserved. Manufactured in Italy.

No part of this book may be used or reproduced in any manner whatsoever without written permission except
in the case of brief quotations embodied in critical articles and reviews. For information address HarperCollins
Children's Books, a division of HarperCollins Publishers, 195 Broadway, New York, NY 10007.

www.harpercollinschildrens.com

ISBN 978-0-06-303617-8

The artist used photocopy and designed paper collage, gouache, acrylic, ink pen, graphite pencil, and gold leaf
to create the illustrations for this book.

Typography by Dana Fritts

22 23 24 25 26 RTLO 10 9 8 7 6 5 4 3 2 1

First Edition

All praises due to the Most Merciful
—J.T-B.

To Ezili, Ava Muriel, the Ancestors, and all the beautiful unborn souls yet to come . . .
Special thanks to Dana, Luana, Jamel, Jamilah,
and ZYEM LLC for the youth model contacts and clothing .
Special thanks also to models Jeremy Kirenkyi, Kourtney Gordon,
Roslyn West, and Vincent Ballentine.
—P.D.

When happy things come to you,
hold them close and never let go.

Hold on to that one time when you just
knew you had slam-dunked the sun!
Keep feeling its fire on your fingertips.

Hold on to new eyes, eyes you've just met,
eyes that have stars of wonder in them—
eyes like yours.

And hold on to eyes—older, wiser, and warm—
that somehow never lost those same stars.

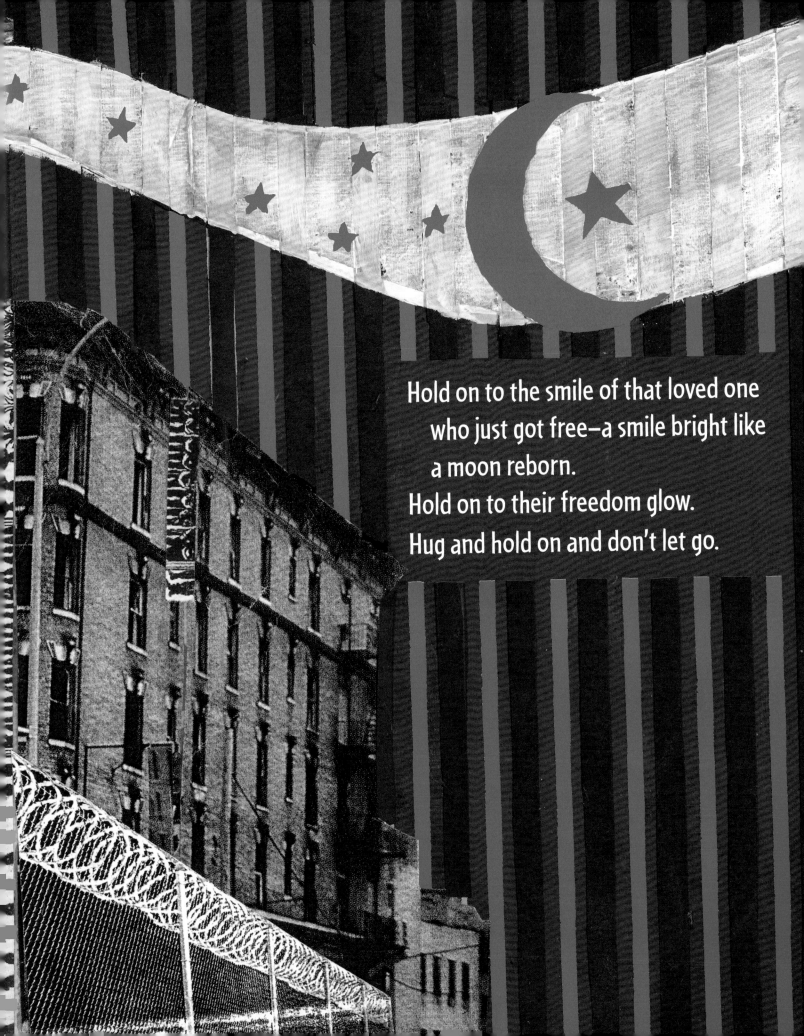

Hold on to the smile of that loved one
who just got free—a smile bright like
a moon reborn.
Hold on to their freedom glow.
Hug and hold on and don't let go.

Hold on to the stories the grown folks tell of your greatness.

Of empires and Wall Streets,
Of Kings and Malcolms,

Of Idas and Sojourners,
Of Hueys and Assatas,

BLACK
WALL STREET

BLACK
WALL STREET
MEMORIAL

Of fighters and poets,

of changemakers and truth-tellers
and the first ones to break through.

You'll need to keep those stories the same way the grown folks kept them.

Close your eyes, wrap your arms around you, and hold on tight.

But when sad things come, you won't want to hold on to those things.
You'll feel like pushing them away.
Some things, you can.

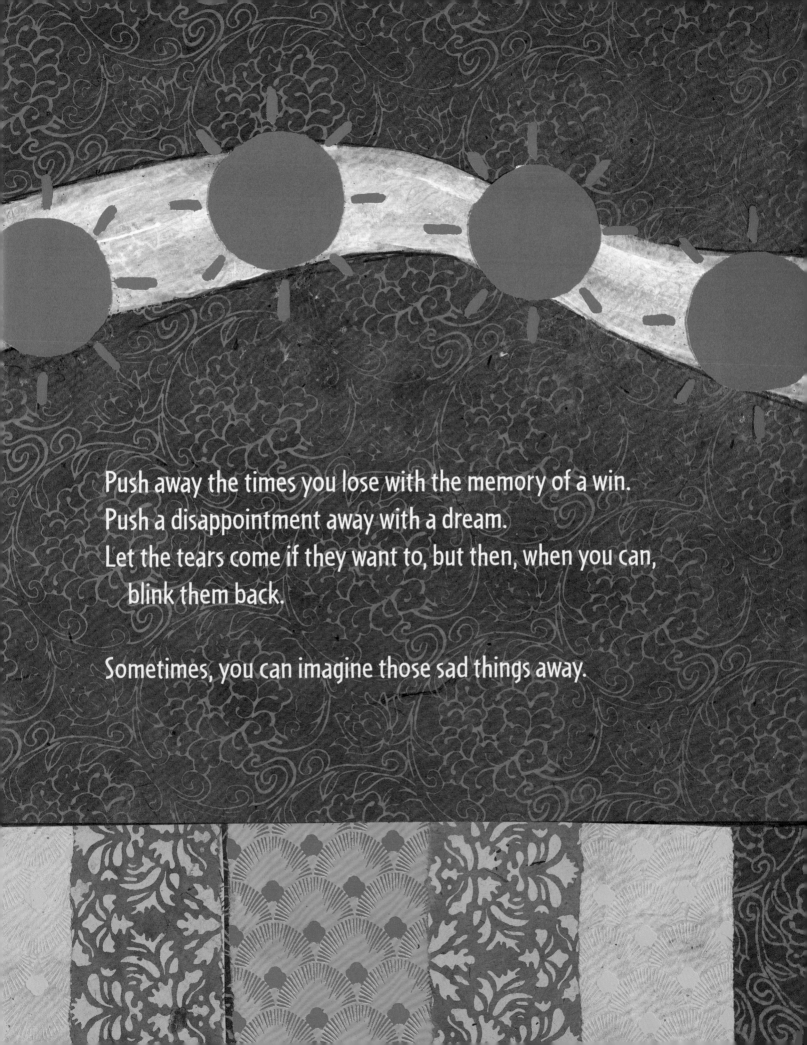

Push away the times you lose with the memory of a win.
Push a disappointment away with a dream.
Let the tears come if they want to, but then, when you can,
   blink them back.

Sometimes, you can imagine those sad things away.

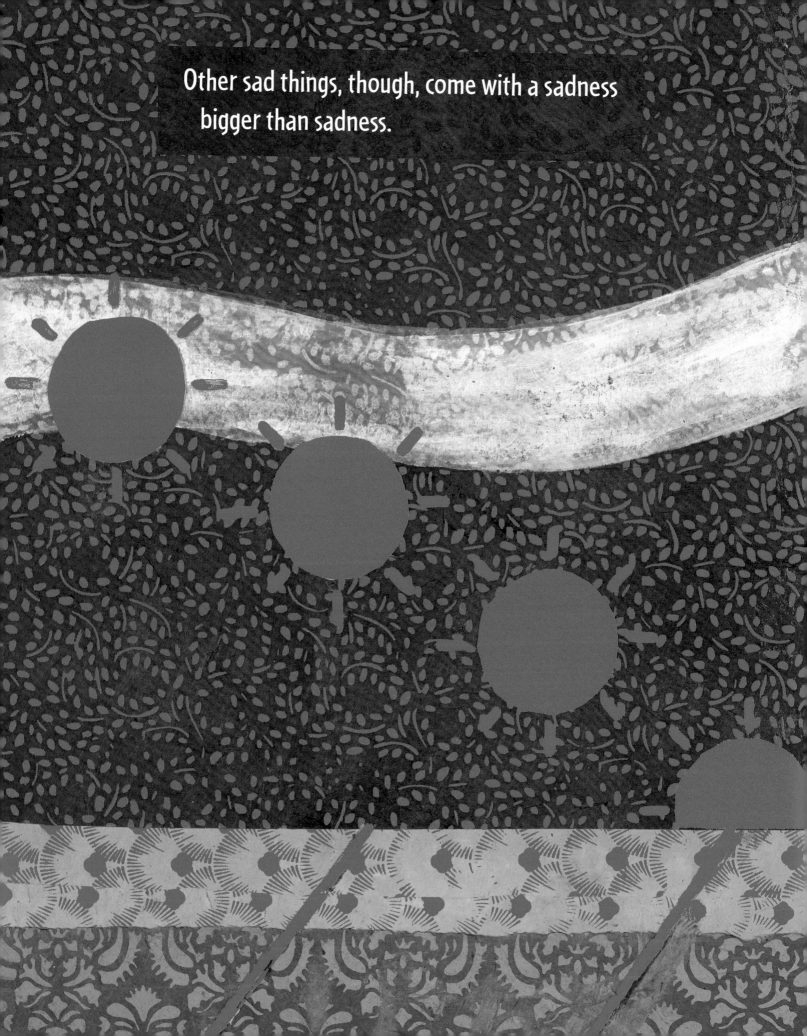

Other sad things, though, come with a sadness
bigger than sadness.

You can't imagine them away.

When the grown folks tell the stories
of our great sadness,
stories of the past
and of today . . .

Let the tears come.
They will need to.
The grown folks might need to let
    their tears come too.
Hug someone if it feels good.
Let out the sad words that get trapped inside.
Those who love you will listen.

Then, look in the mirror, do not blink, and remember . . .

Remember the children from days gone by.
The ones who looked like you.
Don't look away.
See their sad things.

And then . . .

See how they imagined too.
See how they imagined you.
See how they took and made joy however
    and wherever they could.
See their eyes, bright with the light of a drinking gourd.
Those stars twinkle in your eyes too.
See the glow of the sun on their faces
    as they sang "freedom, freedom" in the streets.

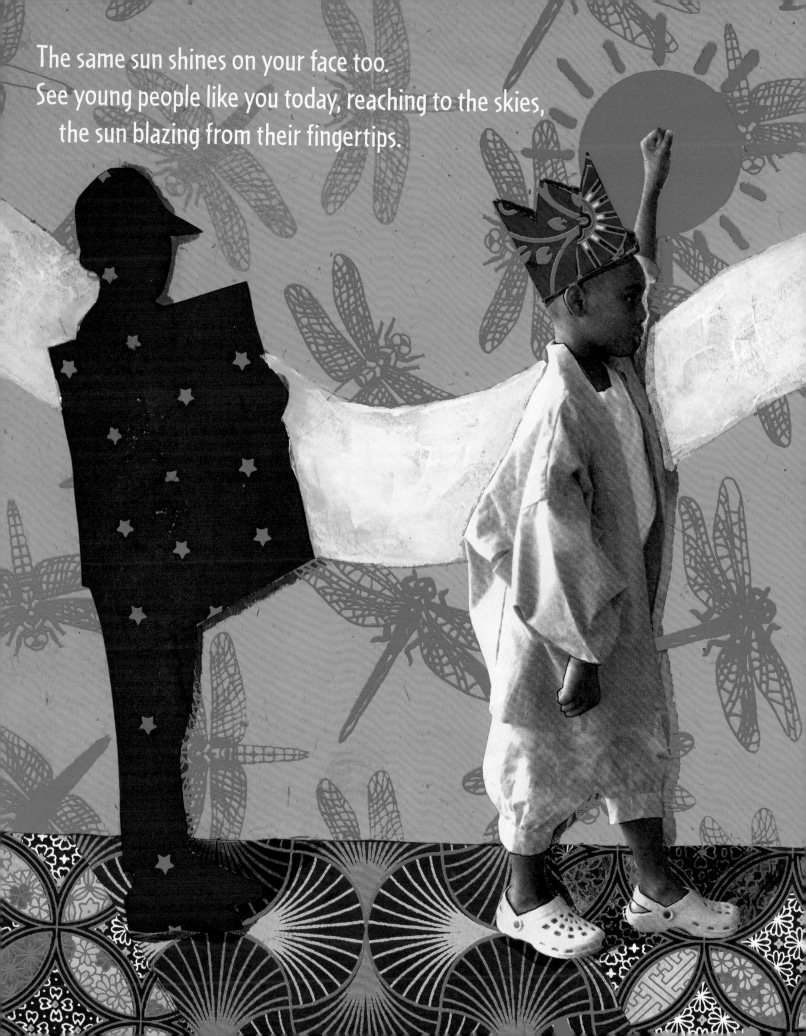

The same sun shines on your face too.
See young people like you today, reaching to the skies,
the sun blazing from their fingertips.

They are shouting that they, that you, that we matter.
From your heart, shout it too.

See them.
See the swirling black winds of their hair and yours.

See how the faces from the past light up the skies
    the way yours lights up the world.
See their might, their brilliance, their victories, their sadness.
See them.
Remember them.

Hold them close and never let go.

AUTHOR'S NOTE

Hold Them Close began as a poem I had fervently written after reading a story about the brutalization of a Black body. What pains me is that I can't recall the story or instance that had brought me to tears then. There are so many people and so many stories. I can't recall which person was brutalized in that moment. What I do recall is the familiar despair I felt and the nagging question that always troubles me when I witness anti-Black violence: How do I talk about this with my Black children?

And within that question are many other questions: How do we reassure Black kids that they are safe in the midst of state-sanctioned terror against their own people? How do we let them know that we as a people are not defined by our pain but rather by our resilience and joy in spite of it? And how do we do all of that while not hiding the stories of oppression in our history? Is there a way to tell them those truths and tell them that there is beauty and strength in their people too?

This book seeks to give some answers through celebrating the extraordinary triumphs of our people. And it seeks to give some answers by offering a hand to hold on tight to as we walk through pain—pain that is past and pain that is very much present.

ILLUSTRATOR'S NOTE

Sister Jamilah's words read like profound poetry to me and went right to my soul. I saw this as a book that would not only be important for young readers but also for the whole family and community. I wanted to create art that would match the seriousness of the text but also honor the bold beauty of the story. I wanted each image in this book to be significant and stunning. To that end, I humbly reached out to one of my personal heroes and a source of great inspiration for me: the iconic photographer Jamel Shabazz. I felt deeply blessed when he enthusiastically agreed to be part of the project.

The beautiful children and adults depicted in this book had never met before the day of the photo shoot, yet within moments they became like a family. I had created a storyboard for the book, and brother Jamel lovingly guided the "family" through the poses for each spread. It was a joyous and harmonious process and I think that shows in the images.

Once the photos were done, I began the process of illustrating, collaging, and painting. The spirit that flows through the pages is meant to symbolize the love, power, and guidance of our ancestors. The gold leaf haloes are meant to depict the divinity within us all and the crowns on the children symbolize the royalty inherent in our children.

I feel deeply blessed and grateful to have been part of this project. I learned and grew so much through the process of creating the art for *Hold Them Close*. My great hope is that the readers will be able to feel my heart and the love that I put into each page of this special book.

BACKGROUND

HOLD ON TO OUR AFRICAN EMPIRES...

Ghana Empire, Soninke: Called "Land of Gold" by Arab traders who wrote of its legendary wealth and military might, this empire flourished between the seventh and thirteenth centuries, controlling the trade of gold and all major goods from Morocco to the Niger River.

Mali Empire: Founded in the thirteenth century by legendary king Sundiata Keita, this empire had an impressive centralized government and one of the world's oldest constitutions: the Kouroukan Fouga.

Songhai Empire: One of the largest African nations ever, its advanced universities attracted scholars from throughout Africa and the Middle East during the fifteenth and sixteenth centuries.

Kingdom of Ife: Considered the birthplace of some of the greatest African art, this kingdom achieved artistic excellence with its bronze, stone, and terra-cotta sculptures between the twelfth and fifteenth centuries.

Kingdom of Benin: This kingdom developed between the fourteenth and nineteenth centuries and organized artists into hierarchies. Europeans stole hundreds of this kingdom's prized brass art pieces, and they are displayed today in European and US museums.

HOLD ON TO BLACK WALL STREET...

Originally called **"Negro Wall Street"** because of its legendary wealth, the bustling all-Black Greenwood district in Tulsa, Oklahoma, was founded in 1906 by former slaves and sharecroppers, with entrepreneur O. W. Gurley purchasing forty acres of land to form the town.

HOLD ON TO DR. KING...

Dr. Martin Luther King Jr. (1929–1968) was a nonviolent activist and Nobel Peace Prize laureate who attained significant legal rulings and protections for Black Americans and other vulnerable populations. His "I Have a Dream" speech is one of the most influential speeches in American history.

HOLD ON TO BROTHER MALCOLM...

Malcolm X (1925–1965), or El-Hajj Malik El-Shabazz, gave voice to Black pride, consciousness, and self-empowerment—ideas that inspired and shaped future Black liberation movements.

HOLD ON TO IDA...

Ida B. Wells-Barnett (1862–1931) was an investigative journalist, suffragette, and groundbreaking civil rights activist and leader who produced some of the most scathing writings against lynching.

HOLD ON TO SOJOURNER...

Sojourner Truth (1797–1883) was an abolitionist, itinerant preacher, and women's rights activist whose "Ain't I A Woman?" speech is famous for its defense of Black women's rights.

HOLD ON TO HUEY . . .

Huey P. Newton (1942–1989) helped form the Black Panther Party (BPP), which challenged police brutality and addressed poverty and inequality in Black communities.

HOLD ON TO ASSATA . . .

Assata Shakur (born 1947) is an ex-political prisoner and former member of the BPP and Black Liberation Army (BLA) whose autobiography details how the FBI and US justice system criminalize Black nationalists.

HOLD ON TO OUR FIGHTERS . . .

Ella Baker (1903–1986) was a civil rights organizer who helped form the Student Nonviolent Coordinating Committee (SNCC). She believed everyday people should be given the skills to stand up to power.

Colin Kaepernick (born 1987) is a quarterback, philanthropist, and activist who kneeled at NFL games during the singing of "The Star-Spangled Banner" to protest police brutality.

Frederick Douglass (c. 1818–1895) became the foremost abolitionist of his time because of his fiery speeches, shocking autobiographies of his enslavement, and nationally read newspaper *The North Star*.

Harriet Tubman (c. 1820–1913) is best known for helping hundreds of people escape slavery. She also supported Union efforts during the Civil War by recruiting Black soldiers and working as a spy.

HOLD ON TO OUR POETS . . .

Maya Angelou (1928–2014) was a prolific poet and author of the acclaimed autobiography *I Know Why the Caged Bird Sings*. She was honored by US presidents for her work.

Gwendolyn Brooks (1917–2000), a writer of politically conscious poetry, was the first Black American to win the Pulitzer Prize and the first Black woman US Poet Laureate.

Gil Scott Heron (1949–2011) recited his Black nationalist poetry in song forms that included percussion, bluesy melodies, and repeating hooks, laying the groundwork for rap music.

Langston Hughes (c. 1902–1967), a leading Harlem Renaissance voice, wrote poetry, plays, short stories, and essays that unapologetically and vividly represented Black culture.

HOLD ON TO OUR CHANGEMAKERS AND TRUTH-TELLERS . . .

James Baldwin (1924–1987) was a writer and activist whose 1963 work, *The Fire Next Time*, is considered a seminal book on race in America.

Oprah Winfrey (born 1954) is a media mogul, actor, and philanthropist whose influence drives everything from book sales to the outcomes of presidential elections.

Aaron Douglas (1899–1979), a leading Harlem Renaissance artist, depicted Black history, culture, aspirations, and struggle in his paintings.

Nina Simone (1933–2003) was an innovative singer and musician whose genre-defying music uplifted Black people and exposed the atrocities of racism.

HOLD ON TO OUR FIRSTS . . .

Arthur Ashe (1943–1993) was the first Black man to win a singles title in tennis in the US Open and at Wimbledon.

Guion Bluford (born 1942) is the first Black person to go to space.

Shirley Chisholm (1924–2005) was the first Black woman elected to the US Congress and the first Black candidate to run for a major political party's presidential nomination.

Bessie Coleman (1892–1926) was the first Black woman pilot.

Ava DuVernay (born 1972) is the first Black woman to win Best Director at the Sundance Film Festival, be nominated for a Best Director Golden Globe, direct a film nominated for a Best Picture Oscar, and direct a film with a budget over $100 million.

Kamala Harris (born 1964) is the first woman US vice president and the first Black American and Asian American to serve in that role.

Thurgood Marshall (1908–1993) was the first Black US Supreme Court justice.

Toni Morrison (1931–2019) was the first Black woman to win the Nobel Prize for Literature.

Barack Obama (born 1961) is the first Black president of the United States.

Sidney Poitier (1927–2022) was the first Black man to win an Academy Award for Best Actor.

Madam C. J. Walker (1867–1919) was the first self-made woman millionaire in the United States.

DON'T LOOK AWAY FROM SLAVERY . . .

The **transatlantic slave trade** was the forced transport and enslavement of ten to twelve million Africans across the Atlantic Ocean. In the United States, enslaved people endured unspeakable abuse for over two hundred and fifty years, including separation from their families and forced, brutal labor.

DON'T LOOK AWAY FROM RACIAL VIOLENCE . . .

Reconstruction Era Backlash: Torturing and murdering thousands, white supremacist groups terrorized Black people to keep them from enjoying their full rights as US citizens after slavery was abolished.

Lynching: Lynching is when a mob rather than a court of law publicly punishes and executes a person, often by hanging, for an alleged crime. At its peak, two or three Black people were lynched each week.

Race Massacres/Riots: White rioters destroyed Black-owned property and hurt and killed hundreds of Black people in East St. Louis, Illinois, in 1917, in several US cities during the "Red Summer" of 1919, in the Greenwood "Black Wall Street" district of Tulsa, Oklahoma, in 1921, and in Rosewood, Florida, in 1923.

DON'T LOOK AWAY FROM JIM CROW . . .

Jim Crow was a system of laws and practices that segregated Blacks from whites in all aspects of life, forced Black people to use lower-quality facilities, and denied them rights as US citizens.

DON'T LOOK AWAY FROM OVERPOLICING . . .

Overpolicing is the unjust, overly aggressive, and inhumane use of prisons and law enforcement to control a population. Black Americans are overpoliced due to concentrated poverty and inequality and discriminatory laws and practices.

SEE THE DRINKING GOURD . . .

The drinking gourd constellation points to the North Star and was used to escape to free northern states or Canada. "Follow the Drinking Gourd" is a song that describes finding freedom this way.

SEE THE CHILDREN'S MARCH . . .

Beginning on May 2, 1963, **the Children's March** was a days-long protest that consisted of young students marching in Birmingham, Alabama. Their efforts helped lead to the passage of the Civil Rights Act of 1964.

SEE THE BLACK LIVES MATTER MOVEMENT . . .

Black Lives Matter is a global network of activists fighting against anti-Black racism and state-sanctioned violence. Its founders are organizers Alicia Garza, Patrisse Cullors, and Opal Tometi, who began the movement with the #BlackLivesMatter hashtag in 2013.

Remember and never let go.

SELECTED SOURCES

I found these sources particularly helpful in the creation of this book. —J.T-B.

Asante, Molefi Kete, and Ama Mazama. *Encyclopedia of Black Studies.* Thousand Oaks: CA: Sage, 2007.

Asim, Jabari, and Lynn Gaines. *A Child's Introduction to African American History: The Experiences, People, and Events That Shaped Our Country.* New York: Black Dog Leventhal, an imprint of Hachette Book Group, 2018.

Bin-Wahad, Dhoruba. "Assata Shakur, Excluding the Nightmare after the Dream: The 'Terrorist' Label and the Criminalization of Revolutionary Black Movements in the USA," edited by Jared Ball, Black Power Media, February 27, 2019, www.imixwhatilike.org/2013/10/15/dhoruba2.

Davis, Thomas J. *History of African Americans: Exploring Diverse Roots.* Santa Barbara, CA: Greenwood, 2016.

"Follow the Drinking Gourd." Pathways to Freedom: Maryland and the Underground Railroad, pathways.thinkport.org/secrets/gourd1.cfm.

Harris, Brandon. "The Most Important Legacy of the Black Panthers." *The New Yorker,* September 5, 2015, www.newyorker.com/culture/culture-desk/the-most-important-legacy-of-the-black-panthers.

"Herstory." Black Lives Matter, www.blacklivesmatter.com/herstory.

Hinton, Elizabeth, LeShae Henderson, and Cindy Reed. "An Unjust Burden: The Disparate Treatment of Black Americans in the Criminal Justice System." Vera Institute of Justice, 2018, www.vera.org/downloads/publications/for-the-record-unjust-burden-racial-disparities.pdf.

"History of Lynching in America." NAACP, December 3, 2021, www.naacp.org/find-resources/history-explained/history-lynching-america.

Holman, Jordyn, and Marisa Gertz. "Black Americans Who Broke Barriers on Wall Street—and Beyond." *Bloomberg,* February 17, 2020, www.bloomberg.com/news/photo-essays/2020-02-17/black-americans-who-broke-barriers-on-wall-street-and-beyond.

Kordak, Mary. "The Art of African Americans." *The African American Years: Chronologies of African-American History and Experience,* edited by Gabriel Burns Stepto, 433–442. New York: Charles Scribner's Sons, 2003.

"Mighty Times: The Children's March." Zinn Education Project, a Collaboration between Rethinking Schools and Teaching for Change, May 2, 2021, www.zinnedproject.org/materials/childrens-march.

Palmer, Colin A. *Encyclopedia of African-American Culture and History: The Black Experience in the Americas.* Detroit: Macmillan Reference USA, 2006.

"The Rise and Fall of Jim Crow." Jim Crow Stories: PBS. Thirteen, 2002, www.thirteen.org/wnet/jimcrow/stories.html.

"West African Kingdoms: The Story of Africa." BBC, BBC World Service, www.bbc.co.uk/worldservice/specials/1624_story_of_africa/page79.shtml.